CLASSIC TALES
ONCE UPON A TIME
THE THREE LITTLE PIGS

THE THREE LITTLE PIGS LIVED WITH THEIR
MOTHER IN THE WOODS. ONE DAY, THEY
REALIZED THEY WERE GROWN UP AND
DECIDED TO LIVE ON THEIR OWN.

WORRIED, THE MOTHER OF THE THREE LITTLE PIGS WARNED THAT THE BIG BAD WOLF LIVED IN THE FOREST AND THAT THEY SHOULD BUILD VERY STURDY HOUSES TO STAY SAFE. THEY SAID GOODBYE TO THEIR MOTHER AND WENT TO LOOK FOR A PLACE TO LIVE.

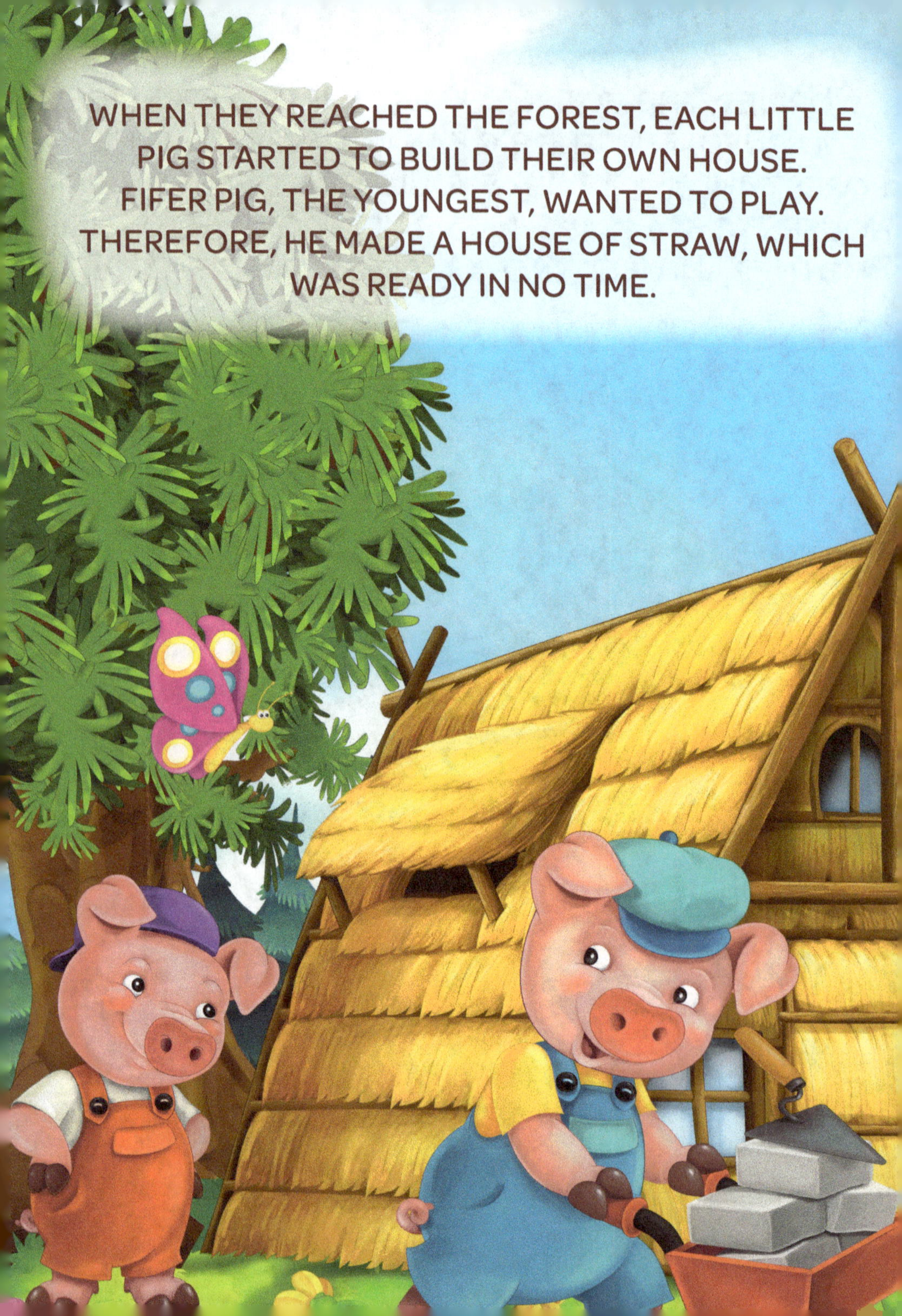

WHEN THEY REACHED THE FOREST, EACH LITTLE
PIG STARTED TO BUILD THEIR OWN HOUSE.
FIFER PIG, THE YOUNGEST, WANTED TO PLAY.
THEREFORE, HE MADE A HOUSE OF STRAW, WHICH
WAS READY IN NO TIME.

FIDDLER PIG, THE MIDDLE SON, EAGER
TO PLAY WITH HIS YOUNGER BROTHER,
GATHERED SOME BOARDS AND BUILT A
WOODEN HOUSE, WHICH ALSO DIDN'T TAKE
LONG TO BE READY.

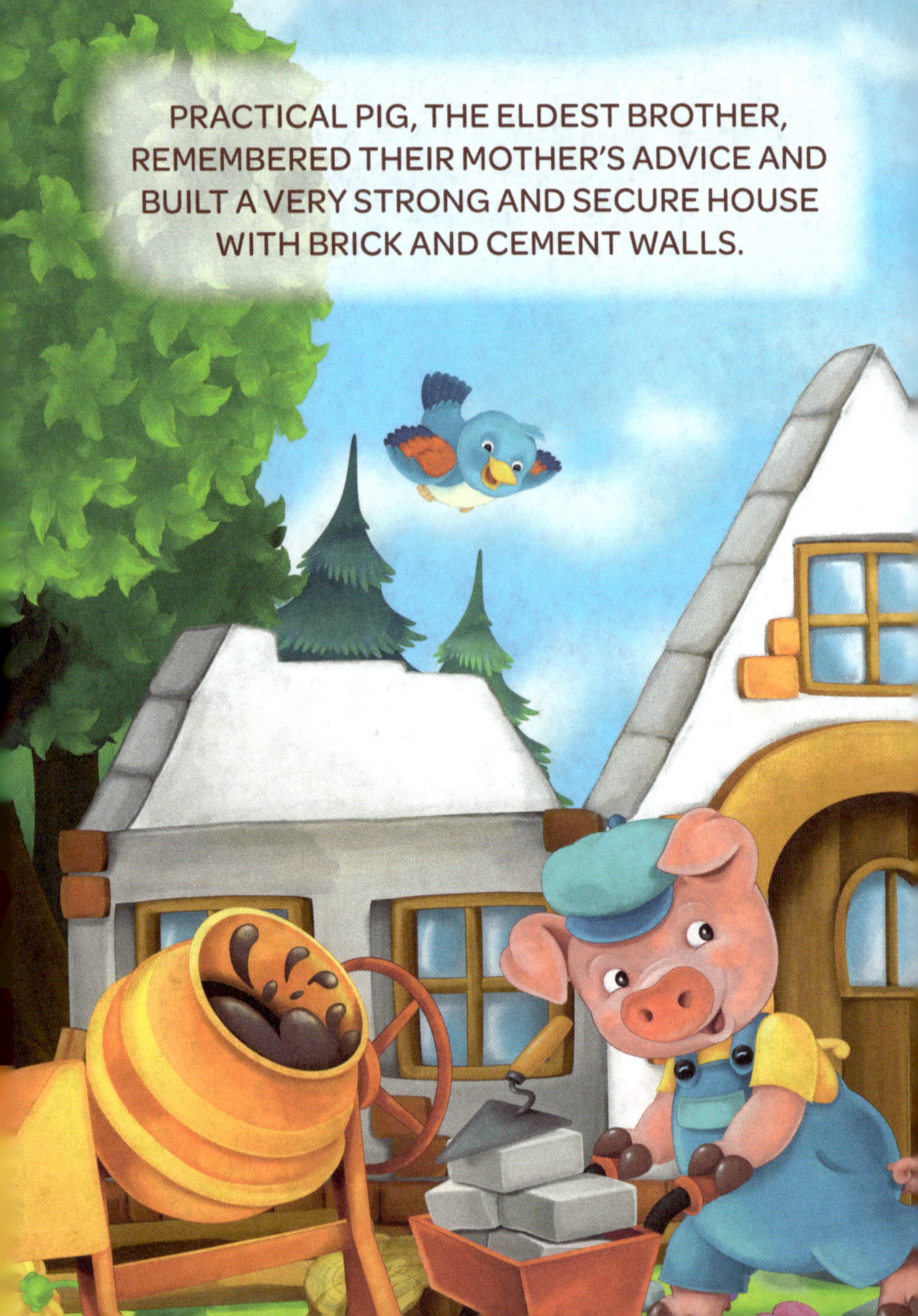
PRACTICAL PIG, THE ELDEST BROTHER,
REMEMBERED THEIR MOTHER'S ADVICE AND
BUILT A VERY STRONG AND SECURE HOUSE
WITH BRICK AND CEMENT WALLS.

DAYS LATER, WHILE FIFER AND FIDDLER PLAYED,
PRACTICAL CONTINUED TO CARRY BRICKS TO
BUILD HIS HOUSE. HE KNEW IT WAS IMPORTANT TO
PROTECT HIMSELF FROM THE BIG BAD WOLF.

WHEN PRACTICAL'S HOUSE WAS FINALLY READY, THE LITTLE PIGS WENT TO PICK DELICIOUS FRUITS IN THE FOREST. SUDDENLY, THE BIG BAD WOLF APPEARED UNDER A TREE AND SAID HE WOULD DEVOUR ALL THREE OF THEM.

TERRIFIED, THE THREE LITTLE PIGS RAN OFF
TO THEIR RESPECTIVE HOUSES, BUT THE
HUNGRY WOLF WENT AFTER THEM.

THE FIRST HOUSE THE WOLF FOUND WAS
FIFER'S. REALIZING THE LITTLE PIG WAS INSIDE,
HE GAVE THREE STRONG BLOWS AND KNOCKED
DOWN THE STRAW WALLS.

DESPERATE, FIFER RAN TO FIGGLER'S HOUSE. HOWEVER, THE HUNGRY WOLF PURSUED HIM, AND, SMELLING THE TWO LITTLE PIGS, GAVE THREE MORE STRONG BLOWS, ALSO KNOCKING DOWN THE WOODEN WALLS.

FIFER AND FIGGLER RAN AWAY FROM THE EVIL ONE AND HID IN PRACTICAL'S HOUSE. THE WOLF WENT AFTER THEM AND STARTED TO BLOW ON THE HOUSE UNTIL HE RAN OUT OF BREATH, BUT NOTHING HAPPENED.

WHEN HE REALIZED HE COULDN'T KNOCK DOWN THE HOUSE, THE WOLF DECIDED TO ENTER THROUGH THE CHIMNEY AND CATCH THE LITTLE PIGS BY SURPRISE.

BUT THE LITTLE PIGS HEARD THE NOISE ON THE ROOF
AND LIT THE CHIMNEY. THE BIG BAD WOLF, UNAWARE
THAT THE FIRE WAS LIT, CONTINUED TO DESCEND.
WHEN HE WAS ALMOST REACHING THE PIGS, HE FELT
HIS TAIL BURNING.

IN GREAT PAIN, THE WOLF RAN OUT OF THE HOUSE WITH HIS TAIL ON FIRE AND WAS NEVER SEEN IN THE FOREST AGAIN.

FIFER AND FIGGLER THANKED THEIR OLDER BROTHER FOR HIS HELP. THEY REALIZED THAT, JUST AS THEIR MOTHER ADVISED, THEY NEEDED TO LIVE SOMEWHERE SAFE. SO, THEY REBUILT THEIR HOUSES WITH BRICKS AND CEMENT, LIKE PRACTICAL'S.

WITH STURDY HOUSES, THE THREE LITTLE
PIGS LOST THEIR FEAR OF WOLVES AND LIVED
HAPPILY EVER AFTER.

THE END